Guided Reading: none

Dear Parent:

Buckle up! You are about to join your child on a very exciting journey. The destination? Independent reading!

Road to Reading will help you and your child get there. The program offers books at five levels, or Miles, that accompany children from their first attempts at reading to successfully reading on their own. Each Mile is paved with engaging stories and delightful artwork.

Getting Started
For children who know the alphabet and are eager to begin reading
• easy words   • fun rhythms   • big type   • picture clues

Reading With Help
For children who recognize some words and sound out others with help
• short sentences   • pattern stories   • simple plotlines

Reading On Your Own
For children who are ready to read easy stories by themselves
• longer sentences   • more complex plotlines   • easy dialogue

First Chapter Books
For children who want to take the plunge into chapter books
• bite-size chapters   • short paragraphs   • full-color art

Chapter Books
For children who are comfortable reading independently
• longer chapters   • occasional black-and-white illustrations

There's no need to hurry through the Miles. Road to Reading is designed without age or grade levels. Children can progress at their own speed, developing confidence and pride in their reading ability no matter what their age or grade.

So sit back and enjoy the ride—every Mile of the way!

For Katherine,
my constant inspiration

Library of Congress Cataloging-in-Publication Data
Thiesing, Lisa.
All better / [written and illustrated] by Lisa Thiesing.
    p. cm. — (Road to reading. Mile 1)
Summary: Despite being a little clumsy at times, Sally the pig enjoys tumbling
through the day.
ISBN 0-307-26111-5 (pbk) — ISBN 0-307-46111-4 (GB)
[1. Pigs Fiction. 2. Clumsiness Fiction.] I. Title. II. Series.
PZ7.T35615A1 2000
[E]—dc21

                                                                99-23996
                                                                CIP

A GOLDEN BOOK • New York
Golden Books Publishing Company, Inc. New York, New York 10106

ISBN: 0-307-26111-5 (pbk)   A MM
ISBN: 0-307-46111-4 (GB)

NOV 03 2000

BW/

ALL BETTER

by Lisa Thiesing

Early one morning,

Sally went to
smell a rose.

And pricked her nose!

Boo-boo.

All better!

Then Sally did a roll.

And fell in a hole.
Boo-boo.

All better!

She tried her tricycle, too.

And off she flew!

Boo-boo.

All better!

Sally climbed a tree.

Whee!

Boo-boo.

All better!

She got ready for bed.

And bumped her head!

Boo-boo.

All better!

Sally woke the next day.

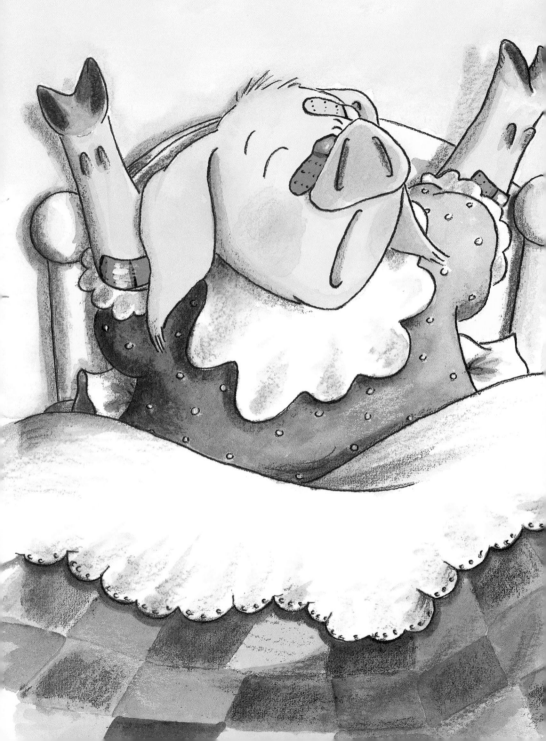

Did her boo-boos
go away?

Hooray!

All better!

Boo-boo.